UPROAR
ON HOLLERCAT HILL

by Jean Marzollo
Pictures by Steven Kellogg

THE DIAL PRESS / NEW YORK

Published by
The Dial Press
1 Dag Hammarskjold Plaza
New York, New York 10017

Design by Atha Tehon
First printing

Library of Congress Cataloging in Publication Data
Marzollo, Jean.   Uproar on Hollercat Hill.
Summary: Petty problems in a cat family escalate into chaos.
[1. Cats—Fiction. 2. Quarreling—Fiction.
3. Stories in rhyme] I. Kellogg, Steven. II. Title.
PZ8.3.M4194Up   811′.5′4 [E]   79-22201
ISBN 0-8037-9027-9   ISBN 0-8037-9028-7 lib. bdg.

The art for each picture consists of a black ink, pencil,
and wash drawing with three color-overlays,
all reproduced as halftone.

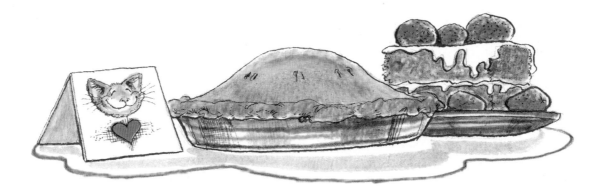

For Kathy and Allen, my sister and brother J.M.

For Colin, a super cat! S.K.

Poppa's drumming,
Children play,

Momma's plowing,
Heavenly day.

Drumsticks breaking,
Train's too wide,

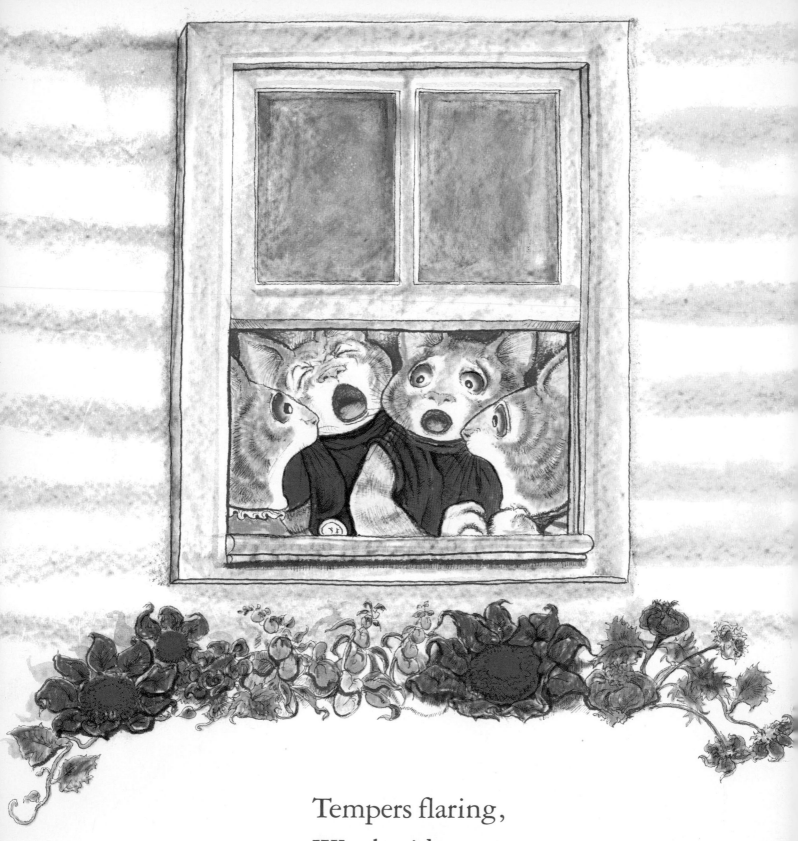

Tempers flaring,
Woe betide.

Strawberry shortcake, huckleberry pie,
I'm gonna punch you in the eye.

Off they're going,
Who knows where,
Momma says,
"Well, I declare."
She forgets
To use the brake—

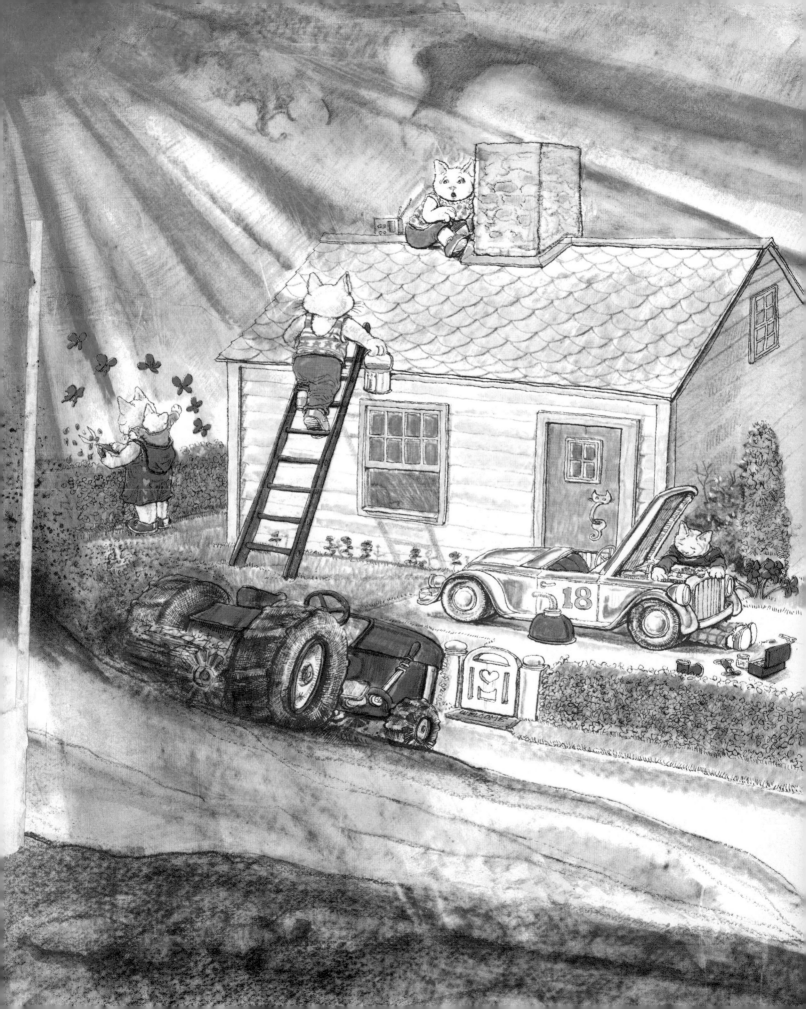

Tractor crashes,
Mercy's sake.

Strawberry shortcake, huckleberry pie,
I'm gonna punch you in the eye.

Now it's raining
On their plight.
Soggy fury:
What a sight.

Poppa finally
Thinks of tea.

Mom finds cookies,
Glory be.

Enter sun
With cheerful rays,
Poppa giggles,
Saints be praised.

Sometimes folks
Just got to fight,
When it's over,
Kiss good night.

Strawberry shortcake, huckleberry pie,
We love you and that's no lie.